For My Michael –
with all my love x ~ CF

For Nicole Ivett –
a real treasure! ~ BC

SIMON AND SCHUSTER
First published in Great Britain in 2012 by Simon and Schuster UK Ltd
1st Floor, 222 Gray's Inn Road, London WC1X 8HB
A CBS COMPANY

A CIP catalogue record for this book is available from
the British Library upon request

ISBN: 978-1-4711-2327-6

Printed in China
3 5 7 9 10 8 6 4

Pirates Love Underpants

Claire Freedman & Ben Cort

SIMON AND SCHUSTER

London New York Sydney Toronto New Delhi

These pirates SO love underpants,
They're on a special quest
To find the fabled Pants of Gold,
For the Captain's treasure chest.

"Anchors aweigh!" the Captain cries,
"Hoist up Black Bloomer's sail!
Unfurl the secret treasure map,
Pants pirates NEVER fail!"

Black Bloomer bobs upon the waves,
The Captain shouts, "Hooray!
Sharks in fancy UNDERPANTS,
We've found Big Knickers Bay!"

The pirates grab their cutlasses,
And row their boats to shore.
But, "Yikes, me hearties, what is this?
Someone's been 'ere before!"

The footprints lead through shifting dunes,
Across the Three Pants Ridge.
Snap! Snap! snarl hungry crocodiles,
Beneath the Long-John Bridge!

The pirates wade through gurgling swamps,
Through caves as black as night.
They trek through prickly undergrowth,
Then, GULP! Oh, what a sight!

"We're here too late!" the pirates gasp.
"ANOTHER pirate crew!
They've found the golden underpants.
What are we going to do?"

The Captain has a cunning plan.
It's clever! It's fantastic!
"Grab their fancy underpants and . . .
CUT through the elastic!"

Sshh! As the rival pirates sleep,
They SNIP round on tip-toe.
But help! The Captain's parrot SQUAWKS,
And wakes them up – Oh no!

"Grab those pants!" the Captain roars.
"They're after us – oooh-arrr!"
But with their pants around their feet,
They don't get very far!

"Yo-ho! Ho-ho!" the pirates dance,
"Fine treasure fills our hold,
But what's the booty we love best?
The glittering PANTS OF GOLD!"

So when you put your pants on, CHECK,
The elastic is in place.
Or like those silly pirates found –
You'll have a bright red face!